DISNEY'S THE LION KING
FRIENDS IN NEED

Adapted by Justine Korman
Illustrated by John Kurtz

A GOLDEN BOOK • NEW YORK
Western Publishing Company, Inc., Racine, Wisconsin 53404

Once upon a time when the Pride Lands were new and the great Lion King Mufasa was still growing, he came upon a little bird in big trouble. The bird was a hornbill named Zazu. And he was about to be cooked by some hungry young hyenas.

Mufasa gave a mighty roar. Well, it wasn't a very mighty roar because he was still a small lion. But it was mighty enough to frighten off the young hyenas.

The little bird introduced himself with a grand bow. Then he said, "Thank you for saving my life, Mufasa. I hope that one day I may be of service to the future Lion King."

Proud Mufasa laughed to himself. How could such a little bird be of any use to a lion?

But the little bird was determined to help somehow.
So he hovered over Mufasa day . . .

and night.

Wherever Mufasa went, Zazu followed.

Mufasa began to feel as if he had grown a second shadow.
"Go away!" the young lion roared.

But Zazu shook his feathered head. "You helped me," he said.
"Now I must help you."

"But you are ruining my hunt!" Mufasa groaned.

"I can help you hunt," Zazu offered. "I will fly up and tell you where the game is."

But the sound of the little bird's wings warned the antelope away.

Zazu even hovered above Mufasa when he wanted to be alone with his future bride, Sarabi.

While the two young lions strolled, the hornbill chattered. "I know everything that happens in the Pride Lands," he bragged. "I see it all from my bird's-eye view. Why, over there your brother, Scar, is teasing a mouse."

"Can't you keep quiet for one minute?" Mufasa asked.

"Of course!" Zazu exclaimed. "Once I didn't say a word for nearly three days. It's a funny story really. You see . . ."

And on the chatter went—until one day Zazu saw several vultures circling above a distant gorge. He pointed out the birds to Mufasa and said, "Shall I fly over to see what's happening, Sire?"

Mufasa yawned. "What does a future king care about ugly, old vultures?" he asked. "There's probably just some small creature over there." Then he settled down for a catnap.

Zazu was too curious to sleep, so he flew over to the gorge. As he got closer, the hornbill saw that the vultures were circling a deep pit and at the bottom stood Sarabi.

The lioness looked up at Zazu and cried, "I can't get out!"

"I will help you!" Zazu screeched. And with a flap of his shiny blue wings he was off.

Zazu flew to Mufasa as fast as he could. Mufasa snapped
wide awake the minute he heard Zazu's news and raced to
the gorge to save his future bride.

But once he had scared away the vultures, Mufasa didn't know what to do. If he climbed into the pit, he would be trapped, too!

"Sire! Over here!" Zazu called. "You can toss down this tree trunk and then Sarabi can climb up."

Mufasa quickly dragged the heavy trunk over to the pit. Then he lowered it down for Sarabi.

In seconds Sarabi climbed to freedom. She rubbed her soft cheek against Zazu and purred, "You saved my life!"

"And you taught me a valuable lesson," Mufasa added.

"The Lion King needs to know everything that goes on in his kingdom, no matter how unimportant it might seem," Mufasa told Zazu.

"I knew you'd come around, Sire," Zazu began. "Why, it was only a matter of . . ."

"I wasn't finished," Mufasa growled playfully. "I have also learned that no creature is so small that he cannot be useful in his own way. Therefore, when I am king, you shall be my adviser. You will fly over the kingdom, tell me everything you see, and alert me to anything that needs my immediate attention."

And that is just what Zazu did for all the years of Mufasa's reign.

"What do you see from up there?" Mufasa called to his new friend.

Zazu chattered, "I see a bright future for King Mufasa and Queen Sarabi, and for their right-paw adviser, Zazu the hornbill!"